D1391961

This book belongs to:

_____

A catalogue record for this book is available from the British Library

Published by Ladybird Books Ltd
80 Strand, London, WC2R 0RL
A Penguin Company

2 4 6 8 10 9 7 5 3 1
© LADYBIRD BOOKS LTD MMVIII
LADYBIRD and the device of a Ladybird are trademarks of Ladybird Books Ltd

ISBN: 978-1-40930-010-6

Printed in China

my favourite

SINGALONG NURSERY RHYMES

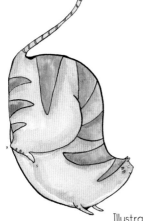

Illustrated by

Miriam Latimer, Holly Surplice,

Natascia Ugliano, Fernando Luiz, Andrew Rowland,

Virginia Allyn, Siobhan Harrison, Kirsteen Harris-Jones

and Kanako Usui

Ride a cock-horse to Banbury Cross,

To see a fine lady upon a white horse;

With rings on her fingers
And bells on her toes,
She shall have music wherever she goes.

Mary had a little lamb,
Its fleece was white as snow;
And everywhere that Mary went
The lamb was sure to go.

It followed her to school one day,
That was against the rule;
It made the children laugh and play
To see a lamb at school.

Baa, baa, black sheep,
Have you any wool?
Yes sir, yes sir,
Three bags full;
One for the master,
And one for the dame,
And one for the little boy
Who lives down the lane.

Here we go round the mulberry bush,
The mulberry bush, the mulberry bush.
Here we go round the mulberry bush
On a cold and frosty morning.

This is the way we wash our hands,
Wash our hands, wash our hands.
This is the way we wash our hands
On a cold and frosty morning.

This is the way we wash our face,
Wash our face, wash our face.
This is the way we wash our face
On a cold and frosty morning.

This is the way we comb our hair,
Comb our hair, comb our hair.
This is the way we comb our hair
On a cold and frosty morning.

This is the way we tie our shoes,
Tie our shoes, tie our shoes.
This is the way we tie our shoes
On a cold and frosty morning.

Lavender's blue, dilly, dilly,
Lavender's green;
When I am King, dilly, dilly,
You shall be Queen.

Roses are red,
Violets are blue,
Sugar is sweet
And so are you.

Rub-a-dub-dub,
Three men in a tub
And how do you think they got there?
The butcher, the baker,
The candlestick-maker,
They all jumped out of a rotten potato;
'Twas enough to make a man stare.

Old King Cole
Was a merry old soul,
And a merry old soul was he;
He called for his pipe,
And he called for his bowl,
And he called for his fiddlers three.

"How many miles to Babylon?"
Three score miles and ten.
"Can I get there by candlelight?"
Yes, and back again.
If your heels are nimble and light,
You may get there by candlelight.

Ding, dong, bell,
Pussy's in the well;
Who put her in?
Little Johnny Green;
Who pulled her out?
Little Tommy Stout.

What a naughty boy was that,
To try to drown poor pussy cat,
Who never did him any harm,
And killed the mice in his father's barn.

Hickory, dickory, dock,
The mouse ran up the clock;
The clock struck one,
The mouse ran down,
Hickory, dickory, dock.

Simple Simon met a pieman
Going to the fair;
Said Simple Simon to the pieman,
"Let me taste your ware."

Said the pieman to Simple Simon,
"Show me first your penny."
Said Simple Simon to the pieman,
"Indeed, I have not any."

Polly, put the kettle on,
Polly, put the kettle on,
Polly, put the kettle on,
We'll all have tea.

Sukey, take it off again,
Sukey, take it off again,
Sukey, take it off again,
They've all gone away.

Pussy cat, Pussy cat,

Where have you been?

"I've been to London

To visit the Queen."

Pussy cat, Pussy cat,

What did you there?

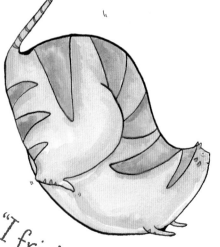

"I frightened a little mouse

under her chair."

Georgie Porgie, pudding and pie,
Kissed the girls
And made them cry;
When the boys came out to play
Georgie Porgie ran away.

Pat-a-cake, pat-a-cake, baker's man,
Bake me a cake as fast as you can.
Pat it and prick it and mark it with B,
Put it in the oven for baby and me.

Half a pound of tuppenny rice,
Half a pound of treacle,
Mix it up and make it nice,
Pop goes the weasel!

Up and down the City Road,
In and out the Eagle.
That's the way the money goes.
Pop goes the weasel!